Albert

The Alphabet Book

P.J. Wright

Magic Rainforest Learning Group

Albert The Alphabet Book

by P.J. Wright

Illustrated by Adit Galih

ISBN 978-0692837023

For my wonderful friends who love adventure. Enjoy!

An ALBERT™ Book

Albert

The Alphabet Book

Once upon a time in a magical rainforest there lived a green, grumpy crocodile. His name was Albert. What do you think Albert liked to do each day?

Albert grew up in the rainforest with his best friend Jade. He liked going on adventures. Jade was a sweet crocodile who liked going on adventures too.

Can you spot Albert and Jade? That's Albert swimming in the water and Jade standing on the beach.

Do you see a monkey? That's Diego. He loves playing on trees.

Are you ready to explore? Let's go!

Aa

Ant

Bb

Butterfly

Cc

Crocodile

Dd

Dragonfly

Ee

Eagle

Ff

Frog

Gg

Gorilla

Hh

Hummingbird

Ii

Iguana

Jj

Jaguar

Kk

Kinkajou

Ll

Leopard

Mm

Monkey

Nn

Nest

Oo

Ocelot

Pp

Parrot

Qq

Queen
Alexandra's Birdwing

Rr

River

Ss

Sloth

Tt

Toucan

Uu

Ulysses
Butterfly

Vv

Viper

Ww

Waterfall

Xx

Xenops

Yy

Yellow
Hibiscus Flower

Zz

Zodiac Moth

What did you see in the rainforest today?

Made in the USA
Monee, IL
06 October 2023

44080397R00021